Faith's Destination

BY

Bob Yandian

Harrison House
Tulsa, OK

Faith's Destination

ISBN 978-1-88560017-2

P.O. Box 55236
Tulsa, OK 74155-1236

Published by:
Harrison House
Tulsa, OK 74145

Cover design by Ed McConnell

Printed in the United State of America

Unless otherwise noted, Scripture quotations are from the New King James Version of the Bible.

Dedication

This book is dedicated to my friend and associate pastor Chip Olin, truly an example of faith in God.

Pastor Bob Yandian

Contents

1

2

1
THE FAITH OF GOD

When most people think of faith, they think of having a trust or faith *in* God, but to some extent, all humans, even those who do not acknowledge God, possess faith. There is a human faith we all share in common. The entire world operates, to some degree, on natural, human faith.

How many times have you walked into a dark room and flipped the light switch, totally expecting the lights to come on? If you're anything like me, you probably enter that familiar room walking straight ahead while reaching for the switch without stopping because you know the lights will come on. My natural, human faith says *I've done this a million times before. The lights are going to come on this time just like they have every other time I've flipped the switch.*

Perhaps you are sitting in your favorite chair without one doubt that your chair will hold you up. You've sat in that same chair and many other chairs over the years with no fear of crashing to the ground. However, could there ever come a day when that seat wouldn't hold you up? Could there ever come a day when you flip on the light switch and it won't work? The answer is yes. In fact, more than likely, over the years that *has* happened. If you have ever sat in a chair that has fallen through, normally you are shocked. *What happened? I can't believe this chair didn't hold me. Who's the crummy guy that made these chairs? It just fell through on me*! Or maybe you have walked into a room, flipped on the light switch, and nothing happened. Perhaps you've taken two paces before you stopped and thought, *What's wrong with these lights? Is the electric company having problems? Did my light bulbs burn out again? I bet a fuse is out. I might have to throw a breaker somewhere.* Put simply, we are surprised if the seat of a chair falls through or when the lights don't work because we trust they will function. Yet, we're usually surprised when our faith in God works even though it is more sure than the greatest human faith!

How many times have you stood in faith, trusting God to bring about His promises, and when they are fulfilled, you're surprised?

The Fig Tree

There is a story in the book of Mark told about Jesus and His disciples. They were staying in the city of Bethany. Every day Jesus and His disciples would go to the city of Jerusalem to minister the Word, but they did not stay in Jerusalem. At the end of each day He and His disciples would walk approximately two miles up the Mount of Olives to the city of Bethany. Every morning as Jesus and His disciples descended the mountain, they would pass through a city on the Mount of Olives called Bethsaida. Fig trees were in abundance and I'm sure Jesus and His disciples would grab the ripe figs to eat for breakfast as they passed through.

One morning as they were passing through Bethsaida, Jesus parted the leaves on a fig tree looking for figs and found nothing but more leaves. He parted those leaves and still found no figs. Then Jesus did something strange. While the disciples were standing around Him, Jesus spoke to the tree!

Mark 11:12-14:

> *Now the next day, when they had come out from Bethany, He was hungry:*
>
> *And seeing from afar a fig tree having leaves, He went to see if perhaps He would find something on it. When He came to it, He found nothing but leaves, for it was not the season for figs.*

> *In response Jesus said to it, "Let no one eat fruit from you ever again." And His disciples heard it.*

When Jesus spoke to the fig tree He said, "No man will ever eat fruit from you ever again!" He then began walking again. Jesus didn't speak these words silently, in His heart. He didn't whisper them. He spoke out loud because this passage tells us the disciples heard Jesus' words.

I can just imagine the disciples looking at one another thinking *Wow! Jesus is talking to trees!* I can imagine them discussing it among themselves, but the Bible doesn't indicate that they ever asked Jesus about it. After Jesus spoke to the tree, it still looked the same. It still had green leaves and a brown trunk, but the next morning as Jesus and the disciples were passing through again, Peter noticed the tree.

Mark 11:20-24:

Now in the morning, as they passed by, they saw the fig tree dried up from the roots.

And Peter, remembering, said to Him, "Rabbi, look! The fig tree which You cursed has withered away."

So Jesus answered and said to them, Have faith in God.

For assuredly, I say to you, whoever ***says*** *to this mountain, Be removed and be cast into the sea, and does not doubt in his heart, but believes that those things he* ***says*** *will be done, he will have whatever he* ***says****.*

Therefore I say to you, whatever things you ask when you pray, believe that you receive them, and you will have them.

The Faith of God is Available

Peter's reaction to the withered fig tree was, "Hey Jesus, look! That tree you cursed is dried up from the roots!" He was totally surprised. Jesus' response to Peter's reaction was, "*Have faith in God.*" What an unusual response! Peter is talking about a dead tree and Jesus says, "Have faith in God." At this moment, Jesus makes a connection between two worlds. In essence He is saying, "The way I caused the natural manifestation in a physical tree was *by faith* in the unseen Creator—God!"

The literal Greek for Jesus' response is "Have the faith *of* God." Many translations bring this out. In other words, "Have the same kind of faith God has." Jesus would not tell us to do this if it was impossible. For us to have the faith of God, it must mean it is available to us. It must mean it is attainable. Think about this, if I wanted to send you to run an errand for me and handed you the keys to my car I could say, "Have the car *of* Bob." That's just old English for "Have Bob's car. Use this car, it's my car and you can use it."

Bible Faith Defined

What exactly is the faith of God? The book of Hebrews defines Bible faith.

Hebrews 11:1-3:

> *Now faith is the substance of things hoped for, the evidence of things not seen.*
>
> *For by it* (faith) *the elders* (Old Testament heroes) *obtained a good testimony.*
>
> *Through faith we understand that the worlds were framed by the word of God, so that things which are seen were not made of things which are visible.*

This verse says, "...*faith is the* SUBSTANCE *of things hoped for, the* EVIDENCE OF THINGS NOT SEEN." Just because faith cannot be seen with our natural eyes does not mean it doesn't exist; it simply means you can't see faith with your physical eyes. In the spirit realm, faith has substance. As far as God is concerned, faith has as much substance as any object does in the natural. Just like we can feel and handle a chair, in the spirit realm God can feel and handle faith; it has substance and it is real. If we could see with our physical eyes into the spirit realm, the substance of faith would appear to us. Verse 3 tells us even the world we live in was framed by God's Word and the things we see are made of what we do not see—God's faith!

Faith is the Bridge

Mark 11:22:

> *So , Jesus answered and said to them, Have faith in God.*

Faith is attributed to God and to *all* of His children. Faith is the bridge between God and man, between the spiritual and natural. It is a product of God. Jesus said, "Have the faith of God." He didn't say to have the faith of Caesar, or Jesus, or Paul, or Matthew. He said, "Have the faith of God." Since God is Spirit, faith must be spiritual.

The World Cannot Understand Faith

The Bible is an instruction book for operating in the spirit realm. This is the reason the world cannot understand it. Those who accept Jesus as Lord have been born twice. Those who have not been born again have only been born one time. They operate in this earth under the world's system, which is backed by the personality of Satan, who is the god of this world. Second Corinthians 4:4 says, "*In whom the god of this world has blinded the minds of them who believe not, lest the light of the glorious gospel of Christ, who is the image of God, should shine on them.*" (KJV)

There are two different words for "world" in the Greek language. The first is *aion*, meaning *age*, which is the "world" used in 2 Corinthians 4:4. This verse, speaking of Satan, could more accurately be translated, "*the god of this* AGE." Satan is only the god of *this* age. When this age is over, Satan will no longer be the *god of this world*. When Jesus returns at the Second Coming, the age of the Millennium will begin and Satan will be banished from earth.

The second Greek word for "world" is *kosmos*, meaning *the world's system or organization*. The English word for "cosmetics" is derived from *kosmos*. Cosmetics is a type of organizing the face. The world is currently operating under an organized system.

John 12:31 says, "*Now is the judgment of this world: now shall the prince of this world be cast out.*" (KJV) The Greek word for "world" in this verse is *kosmos*. Satan is called the prince of the *kosmos*. Jesus said, "*...the prince of this world's system will be cast out.*"

John 14:30 says, "*Hereafter I will not talk much with you: for the prince of this world comes, and has nothing in me.*" (KJV) Again, the word *kosmos* is used for "world." Jesus said, "*...for the prince of this world's system cometh.*"

John 16:11 says, "*...the prince of this world is judged.*" (KJV) Satan, the prince of this *world system*, is judged.

Satan is not only the god of this age, he is the god of this world's system or organization.

The World's System

The world is operating under a system. Before we were born again, we entered this world's system simply by being born. Birth entitles us to operate under the system of the world. In this system, Satan has attempted to emulate God to meet the basic needs of man. God offers man fulfillment, freedom, relationship, protection, health, and prosperity. Satan has a counterfeit for each one of these. God created man to express himself in worship, so Satan offers religion. Man needs protection and God provides angels to protect him. The world offers man an insurance plan. God gives man divine health. The world provides doctors, hospitals, and medicine. Aside from religion, none of these things are bad, but they cannot compare to what God has provided for mankind.

If we had never been born into this world, we could have never been born into God's kingdom. If it hadn't been for the world's system or organization, many of us might have died prematurely. At one time or another, most of us have gone to a doctor who has helped us, but the more we grow in God, the more we should depend on Him. There is more power in one scripture than there is in all the doctors in the earth combined! God offers prosperity. The world's system says put your money in a savings account and receive interest on it. God's system is always better than the world's system.

Operating in God's System

How do we begin to operate in God's system? Just as we were born into this world, entitling us to operate in this worlds' system, we must be born into God's kingdom to operate in His system. We must be born a second time—born again. Some have been born a second time, but have never taken advantage of God's system. They are still operating in the world's system.

Everything we have learned in the world's system is in accordance with our natural birth. Schoolbooks, magazines, newspapers, television, the internet, everything programs us in the natural and teaches us about the world's system. God's system operates differently than the world's. There is only one way to learn about God's system and it is found in the Word of God. As we study and follow the teachings in the Bible, we learn that what the world has taught has not always been correct. The world says the way to get money is to save and invest it; God says to give it away. This doesn't make sense to our mind because our mind has been trained by the world's system. It needs to be renewed.

The more intimately you come to know God and the deeper your commitment to Him, the less options you will have. As you grow closer to the Lord, there will be some things you were once permitted to do, that you will no longer be able to do if you want to continue to grow. For instance, maybe you have been challenged with headaches and have taken a certain medication every time a headache flares up. There is nothing wrong with taking medicine, but you may reach a point in your walk with the Lord where He will require you to stand in faith on His promises for the headache to go away rather than taking the medicine you have always used.

Banks are fine, credit cards are fine, and medicine is fine. These things are good and part of the world system in which we live and operate each day. But what will you do if the banks go under like many did during the Great Depression? God's system is not based upon what happens on Wall Street; it's not based on inflation or recession. God's system is based on *His riches in glory by Christ Jesus*, and heaven will *never* have an economic depression!

Proof for Our Mind

The Bible is a supernatural book, and if a person has not been born again, he or she cannot understand it. A person without the new birth tries to read and understand it with their mind, like any other book. But if you try to read it without the revelation of the Holy Spirit, it won't make sense. First Corinthians 1:18 says, "*For the message of the cross is to foolishness to those who are perishing;*

but to us who are being saved it is the power of God."

As Christians, we must not approach the Word of God with our mind either. If I am standing on God's promise for healing from a cold, my mind may be fighting against me because of the symptoms, but my experience of being healed of colds in the past says the promise of healing *does* work. You may be standing on God's Word for healing, finances or any number of promises found in His Word, and your mind might be screaming, "This doesn't work!" This is the time to remember all the other times you stood on God's promises and saw them come to pass. One way we can renew our mind is by seeing God's Word work over and over again. Our mind needs that proof. Don't get me wrong, the Word works whether your mind believes it or not, but by reflecting on how He has come through in the past encourages our faith as we are standing for the next manifestation in our life.

Everything Produces After its Own Kind

Every born again believer has faith. Romans 12:3 says, "*...think soberly, as God has dealt to each one the* MEASURE OF FAITH." SECOND PETER 1:1 says, "*...to those who have obtained* LIKE PRECIOUS FAITH *with us by the righteousness of God and our Savior Jesus Christ.*" God starts every believer at the same level of faith. He wasn't more generous with one person than He was with another. We have all been given *like precious faith* and the *measure of faith*.

If faith is an attribute of God, how did we obtain faith? Where did the measure of faith come from? We had to be born of God. In John 3:6 Jesus told Nicodemus, "*That which is born of the flesh is flesh; and that which is born of the Spirit is spirit.*" Jesus was simply bringing out a law that was established in Genesis: *Everything produces after its own kind.* Flesh produces flesh. Spirit produces spirit. Your physical attributes are a result of earthly parents. If you plant corn, you get corn. If you plant wheat, you get wheat. You can't plant cucumber seeds and expect tulips to come up. This is a natural law. Cats produce cats, elephants produce elephants, and people produce people. God produces spirits because He is a Spirit. In God's system, if you plant love, you will receive love. If you sow money into God's kingdom, you will receive a financial return.

Growth Potential

When you were born, the potential to grow from a baby into an adult was within you. You had newborn hands, which grew into toddler hands, which grew into school-age hands, which grew into teenage hands, which finally grew into adult hands. Within your physical body was the capability to increase to the size it is today. That potential existed when you were born. Similarly, you don't need to pray for more faith. The faith you were given at the new birth has the capability within itself of increasing.

Think about the day babies discover their hands. They examine them, turn them over. You can almost imagine what is going through their little minds, "What are these? Where did these come from?" Yet, a baby is born with its hands! In the same way, once you are born again, you have faith. You may not discover that fact for awhile. You may spend time praying for what you have already been given and have not yet discovered, but it is already yours!

When you were first born, your hands couldn't hold a bottle, your eyes couldn't focus, and your feet couldn't hold you up. But those same hands now drive a car, those same eyes can now read a book, and those same feet can now walk and even run. Did we learn to do these things overnight? No. We stumbled, repeatedly made mistakes, but through use we became proficient at all of these things.

When you were born of God, you received all of His attributes. Everything you need to operate in His system has been given to you. God will not be adding anything else. He has already put within you the ability to increase in faith, in love, in peace, in joy, in every attribute of God. Just as we continue growing and learning in the natural, we can continue growing in God.

Getting Faith from the Inside to the Outside

We have the faith of God. It is on the inside. How do we get faith that is on the inside to the outside where we really need it? Jesus told us how: "*For assuredly, I say to you, whoever* ***says*** *to this mountain, Be thou removed, and be thou cast into the sea, and does not doubt in his heart, but believes that those things he* ***says*** *will be done, he will have whatever he* ***says****. Therefore I say to you, whatever things you ask when you pray,* *believe that you receive them, and you will have them*" (Mark 11:23-24).

The way to release the faith inside you is by *speaking*. Once you release your faith through the words of your mouth, you will have taken your faith from the inside to the outside and it can begin to produce. Seed does no good if it remains in the sack. It must be removed from the sack and planted in the ground before it can produce. Faith is the same. It does no good if it remains resident within you. We must be doers of the Word by planting seed—speaking the Word. Once the seed is planted, it is in a place where it can produce.

Another way to plant the seed of faith is to believe you receive *when* you pray. The Word of God assures us when we plant that seed by faith and water and feed it with our confession, it will produce!

The Language of Faith

Not only does everything produce after its kind, everything has a voice or language characteristic to its nature. Cats meow because they have a cat nature. Dogs bark because they have a dog nature. Chickens cluck because they have a chicken nature. Babies coo and cry because they have a human nature.

Once we are born again, we receive the language of the inner man from our Heavenly Father. The language of your born again spirit calls those things which be not as though they were, just like our Heavenly Father. Abraham had faith in God, it was accounted unto him for righteousness, and he began to express the voice of his inner man, "I am the father of many nations, just as God has said," even though nothing in the natural looked like he would ever be the father of one child through his wife Sarah, let alone the father of many nations! Abraham's spirit man called those things which be not as though they were.

Jesus said we are to *speak* to the mountain while there is no evidence it is ever going to move. This is when we speak. This is the voice of faith, the voice of the inner man. Abraham believed and confessed he was the father of many nations *before* Sarah became pregnant. He called those things which be not as though they were, and they came to pass!

Speaking in faith should be natural to the born again believer. Confessing things that have not yet manifested should be natural because faith is the language of our Heavenly Father. At the moment of our salvation, we received faith. How was the earth created? *God spoke.* How did the planets come into existence? *God spoke.* God speaks of those things which be not as though they were and we have inherited the language of faith from Him!

If you are straining in your faith, you're probably out beyond your level of faith. Faith is not a blind leap into the unknown. Faith rests with assurance in the promises of God and steps out confidently on God's Word.

How Faith Comes

Romans 10:17:

> *So then faith cometh by* HEARING, *and* HEARING *by the word of God.*

Notice in this verse, *hearing* is mentioned twice. Faith does not come only by hearing with our physical ears, we must also hear with our inward ears. There were a number of occasions when Jesus said, "*He that hath ears to hear, let him hear.*" Jesus was inferring it is possible to have physical ears and not hear. Romans 10:17 could better be translated, "*Faith comes by understanding the Word of God.*" When we gain understanding of the Word of God, faith increases with that understanding. Whenever a biblical truth is revealed to you in your spirit and you comprehend that part of the Word, faith comes with that understanding.

2

THREE COOPERATING POWERS WITH FAITH

There are three powers that cooperate with faith: hope, patience, and love. Faith is a link between you and God. God is on one end, you are on the other, and faith connects you together. When you believe God and step out in faith on one of His promises, there is a divine link which is invisible to the natural eye, but is a spiritual substance called faith. Faith reaches into the unseen spirit world, grabs hold of God's promises, and brings the manifestation of those promises into this natural world.

Romans 5:1-5:

> *Therefore being justified by faith, we have peace with God through our Lord Jesus Christ:*
>
> *By whom also we have access by faith into this grace in which we stand, and rejoice in* HOPE *of the glory of God.*
>
> *And not only so, but we glory in tribulations also: knowing that tribulation works* PATIENCE.
>
> *And patience, experience; and experience,* HOPE*:*
>
> *And hope makes not ashamed; because the* LOVE *of God is shed abroad in our hearts by the Holy Ghost was given to us.* (KJV)

Verse 2 says we "*rejoice in* HOPE." Hope is the first cooperating power with faith. Faith and hope work hand in hand. Verse 3 says *"tribulation works* PATIENCE." Patience is the second cooperating power. Verse 5 says, "...*hope makes not ashamed; because the* LOVE *of God is shed abroad in our hearts by the Holy Ghost.*" Love is the third power that cooperates with faith.

Faith does not stand by itself between you and God. It is supported by three guy-wires. One wire is hope. The second wire is patience. The last wire is love. Think about the guy-wires on a large antenna. What would happen if one of its guy-wires were to break? It would become unstable and probably fall to the ground. The devil cannot get to your faith because it is located in your spirit, the inward man, part of the new creation on the inside. Instead, he will try to weaken the powers that cooperate with your faith. If he can get you to give up hope, lose your patience, or stop walking in love, it can negatively affect your faith. All of God's faith and power may be available to you, but if the devil can affect your hope, patience, or love, neither faith nor power will work in your life.

Faith and Hope

Abraham, the father of our faith, not only operated in faith, he also operated in godly hope.

Romans 4:17-18:

> *(As it is written, I have made thee a father of many nations,)* BEFORE *him whom he believed, even God, who quickens the dead, and calls those things which be not as though they were.*
>
> *Who against* HOPE *believed in* HOPE, *that he might become the father of many nations, according to that which was spoken,* SO SHALL YOUR SEED BE. (KJV)

We know faith comes by hearing the Word of God, but Abraham did not have the Word of God, he did not have a Bible. Abraham couldn't open to Mark 11:23-24 because it didn't exist. Abraham received faith by observing God. The word "before" in verse 17 in the Greek means *face to face with.* Abraham put himself face to face with God and observed everything God did. God called those things that be not as though they were, so Abraham began to do the same. Even though he and his wife, Sarah, were too old to have a child, Abraham kept confessing, "I am the father of many nations." By patterning himself after God, Abraham developed faith.

Notice, HOPE is mentioned twice in verse 18. Just as there are two types of faith, there are two types of hope. There is a natural hope and there is a supernatural hope. When doctors say, "There is no hope," God says, "Yes, there is." Godly hope comes from the same place godly faith comes from—the Word of God. Verse 18 makes the statement,

"So SHALL thy seed be." Is "shall" past, present, or future? Future. Hope is *always* future.

Hebrews 11:1 says, "*Now faith is the substance of things* HOPED *for, the evidence of things not seen.*" There are times when a dream can seem so real, but a dream has no substance. Hope is like a dream, a goal, a target set before you. You must pull out the arrow of faith and aim it at the target of hope. Mark 11:24 could read, "*What things you* HOPE *for when you pray, believe that you receive them and you will have them.*" The New English Bibles says, "*Now faith is giving substance to hope.*" In and of itself, hope has no substance. Faith feeds hope and gives it substance, but without hope, faith has nothing to feed. Without faith, hope will remain without substance. It is important to have a vision or dream, but faith is necessary for that vision or dream to come to pass.

Where do we get vision? Where do we get hope? From the Word of God. Hope says, "You want to be healed? There's a plan in the Word of God that will get it for you." As you meditate on the hope of healing, your hope takes on substance and the healing manifests in your body.

It is possible for the devil to steal your hope. How? Because hope is part of the soul, part of the mind.

1 Thessalonians 5:8:

> *But let us who are of the day be sober, putting on the breastplate of* FAITH *and* LOVE, *and as a helmet the* HOPE *of salvation.*

Notice, all three cooperating powers of faith are mentioned in this verse. Faith and love is the breastplate, but hope is the helmet. What does the helmet protect? Our mind, and the mind is part of the soul.

Most buildings are regulated with a thermostat. Now within that little thermostat box there is absolutely no power. The thermostat is the goal setter. The real power is in the air conditioning or heating unit. Our mind is nothing but a goal setter. It has no power. We use our mind to get into the Word of God, discover what He has promised us, then we set our minds on what God has said. Once we do—BOOM—the power of God comes and causes the Word we have set our mind on to come to pass, to take on substance.

Conversely, if we decided to remove the thermostat from the wall, the air conditioning and heating units may be available with the power to produce, but there is nothing there to set the goal. We must have hope, produced by the Word of God, for the manifestation because hope works in conjunction with faith.

Whenever you hear the Word of God, it enters your mind and produces hope which then enters your spirit and produces faith. When the Word is released and you act on faith, your faith gives your hope substance.

Hope is in the Future

Hebrews 6:17-20:

Thus God, determining to show more abundantly to the heirs of promise the immutability of his counsel, confirmed it by an oath:

That by two immutable things, in which it was impossible for God to lie, we might have a strong consolation, who have fled for refuge to lay hold of the hope set before us:

This hope we have as an anchor of the soul, both sure and steadfast, and which enters the Presence behind the veil,

Where the forerunner has entered for us, even Jesus, having become High Priest forever according to the order of Melchizedek.

Verse 18 says hope is *set before us.* Again, hope is in the future; it is the goal you *see.* When you *see* yourself delivered from financial bondage, free from sickness and disease, the manifestation is on the way!

Verse 19 says hope is *an anchor of the soul.* The purpose of an anchor is to keep a ship from drifting. When we are standing in faith, hope keeps us anchored. Satan wants us to become double-minded and confused so we won't receive anything from God, but hope will keep us from drifting away from the promises of God.

Verse 19 tells us the anchor in within the veil. In other words, the anchor of hope is secured on the other side of the veil. Verse 20 calls Jesus the *forerunner.* The terms *veil* and *forerunner* relate to the ships of that day. When a ship would enter a harbor, there might be fog or a *veil.* When there was fog, the sailors couldn't see past the veil of fog to see whether there were rocks between the ship and the shore. In these cases, a *forerunner* would be sent to stand in front of the ship. He would grab a rope attached to the ship, dive into the water, and begin to swim toward the shore. As the forerunner headed for the shore, he would watch for rocks that might hinder the ship from coming safely to shore. Once the forerunner disappeared beyond the veil of fog, he would swim to the shore and tie the rope securely around a large rock, yanking out the slack and signaling to the crew he had safely arrived on shore. At this point, the entire crew would jump into the water at the front of the ship, grab the rope and begin to pull. As they pulled, the ship would be guided safely through all the rocks the forerunner had already passed through.

Jesus is the forerunner who has gone to the throne room of Heaven. He has gone from this natural world and disappeared through the veil into the spiritual world, but He took the rope with Him and securely tied it around the throne of God. At the other end of the rope of hope is faith. One day we will give our last pull and we will arrive at the throne room of God! Obstacles may come, but Jesus has already gone through and the rope is secure. The only way we can fail is to let go of the rope! Hope is in the future, but what connects us to future hope is the rope of faith.

You may be hoping in the promises of God, "I believe I receive. With His stripes I was healed. Himself took my infirmities and bare my sicknesses." Each day you pull on that rope, until one day, your manifestation arrives. One day, you'll pull up to shore. You'll come to the edge of your hope, and your faith will have given your hope substance!

Faith and Patience

Romans 5:3:

> *And not only that, but we also glory in tribulations, knowing that tribulation produces* PATIENCE.

This verse does not say we are to glory *for* tribulations; we are to glory *in* tribulations. James 1:2-3 says, "*...count it all joy when you fall into various trials. Knowing that the testing of your faith produces* PATIENCE." Counting it all joy doesn't mean you have to stand up and praise God *because of* the trial. We glory *in* tribulation. Why? Because tribulation produces patience.

PATIENCE IS THE POWER OF FAITH. HOPE IS THE GOAL OF FAITH. LOVE IS THE PROTECTOR OF FAITH. Patience is the power that causes your faith to manifest. Satan probably comes against patience more than any other area and the only way he can bring opposition against patience is through tribulation. I can guarantee, every time you step out in faith, tribulation is headed your way. You were no threat to the devil until you decided to step out in faith.

The King James Version says, "*...tribulation worketh patience.*" The Greek word for "worketh" in this verse is *works out*. This verse is *not* saying tribulation brings the patience out of you. Tribulation is the circumstance or opportunity for you to allow patience to work itself out. It is useless to pray for patience. The only thing that will cause patience to manifest in your life is tribulation.

James 1:2:

> *My brethren,* COUNT IT ALL JOY
> *when you fall into various trials,*

In the Greek, the phrase "count it all joy" means *throw a party*. This is the closest meaning in the English we can find for this phrase. What are we supposed to do when Satan comes against us with trials and tribulations? Throw a party! You talk about throwing confusion at Satan.

James 1:3-4:

> *Knowing that the testing of your faith produces patience.*
>
> *But let patience have its perfect work, that you may be perfect and complete,* LACKING NOTHING.

Patience can bring you to the place where you *lack nothing* because all of the manifestations have taken place. The force of patience brings you from the point of believing you receive to the manifestation.

James 1:12-13:

> *Blessed is the man who endures temptation; for when he has been approved, he shall receive the*

> *crown of life, which the Lord has promised to those that love him.*
>
> *Let no one say when he is tempted, I am tempted by God; for God cannot be tempted with evil, nor does He Himself tempt anyone.*

When you have stood in faith and patience and the manifestation finally comes, the Bible calls you *blessed!*

Don't Blame God

One of Satan's tactics when you are in the midst of a temptation or trial is to get you to blame God for what you are going through. James is saying, "Don't blame God when you are in the midst of a temptation or trial." The most difficult time to continue standing in faith is when you are under pressure. God does not try your faith. Satan tries your faith. The devil is not omniscient. He doesn't know tomorrow nor does he know how you will respond in certain situations. Satan simply sends trials and persecution. He applies pressure to see what will come out of the inside of you, whether it's doubt and frustration or whether you will continue to stand on God's Word. When the devil puts the pressure on, it is an opportunity for patience to be manifested in your life!

Hebrews 6:12 says with *faith and patience* we will inherit the promises of God. There is an inheritance in every promise, but what pulls that inheritance from the spirit realm to the natural realm is faith and patience. The more patience manifests itself, the shorter the time period between when you believe and when the promise is manifested.

Faith and Love

The third cooperating power with faith is love. The Bible says faith "*works by love*" (Galatians 5:6). Fear is the opposite force of faith. What does the Bible say casts out fear? Perfect love.

When God's love is operating with your faith, fear has no entrance into your life. Fear always produces torment (1 John 4:18) and nullifies faith. God's love is like an army surrounding your faith keeping fear out of your life. As long as you are operating in love, fear can have no dominion in your life and your faith will be unhindered.

The Bible says, "...*now abide faith, hope, love, these three; but the greatest of these is love*" (1 Corinthians 13:13). Why is love the greatest? The Bible never says God is faith. The Bible never says God is hope. However, the Bible does declare that GOD IS LOVE.

The Rich Young Ruler

In Matthew 19 and Mark 10 we are told the story of the rich young ruler. Mark 10:17 says, "*Now as He was going out on the road, one came running, knelt before Him, and asked Him, Good Teacher, what shall I do that I may* INHERIT *eternal life?*"

This young man was religious and being religious, he was really not interested in finding out how to have eternal life. Like many religious people, he was proud of his good works and thought they would guarantee him an entrance into heaven. What this young man really wanted was for Jesus to pat him on the back and tell him what a great job he was doing. His question to Jesus reveals he believed he could *do* something to get to heaven. Religious people always want to *do* something. There is absolutely nothing wrong with working for the Lord if you are working with the right motives, but *you cannot work your way to heaven.* I don't work to try to *get* to heaven; I work because I'm *going* to heaven.

This man asked Jesus, "What should I do to *inherit* eternal life?" What he was asking Jesus was a total contradiction because we are *born* into an inheritance; we don't *do* something to gain what already belongs to us! I would wonder what was wrong if my son wanted to work for something that already belonged to him.

This rich young ruler believed he must keep the law, and all of the commandments, to enter heaven. He was trying, with his own self-effort, to get into heaven. Jesus uses a debater's technique with the man. He said, "If you want to get to heaven, you must keep the commandments." Jesus went through the Ten Commandments and suddenly recited Leviticus 19:18, "*But you shall love thy neighbor as yourself.*" Jesus had a right to do this because the law is not just the Ten Commandments. The law also includes the first five books of the Old Testament. Amazingly, this young man said, "I've kept them all since I was a youth. What else do I need to do?" I'm sure he expected Jesus to say, "Wow! I've never met anyone like you before! Aren't you a wonderful young man?" Instead, Jesus said, "Okay, then sell everything you have and follow Me." In essence, Jesus was saying to him, "If you really love your neighbor as yourself, sell everything you own and give it to the poor." The young man walked away. Jesus proved to him he couldn't keep that one commandment, and under the law, breaking *one* commandment was breaking all the commandments.

The Eye of the Needle

Matthew 19:24-25:

> *And again I say to you, It is easier for a camel to go through the eye of a needle, than for a rich man to enter the kingdom of God.*
>
> *When his disciples heard it, they were greatly astonished, saying, Who can be saved?*

As the young man walked away, Jesus' disciples were amazed at what Jesus said to them. They were thinking *If a rich man can't enter heaven, who can?* However, they didn't understand what Jesus was saying. When we think of a camel going through the eye of a needle, we think of a sewing needle. However, Jesus was referring to something else. During Jesus' day, a high protective wall surrounded most cities. The walls of the city were joined by two large double gates, which were the entrance into the city. These gates were so wide, twenty people could enter the city side-by-side. Sitting on top of the wall was the watchman. He would keep a watch on the surrounding desert and would warn the city of any approaching enemy armies. Each night the front gates would be closed. However, there was a small gate within one of the large gates called *the eye of the needle*. The gate was so small, only one person could enter at a time. When a traveler would enter a city at night with his camel loaded down with saddle bags, the problems began. To get the camel through that small door was very difficult. The camel would have to be on its knees, the bags and saddle removed, and several people would have to try to push it through that little door. I can imagine one person pulling at the front and another pushing at the back, and maybe two others pressing in the camel's sides to get it through that small gate. Then all the bags, goods, and saddle had to be passed through the gate. Once the camel was finally on the other side of the gate, it had to be reloaded with the saddle and all the bags that had been removed.

What was Jesus saying to the rich young ruler? If he would just drop his treasure outside and go through the little door of salvation, Jesus would make sure he received his treasures on the other side. Just a few verses later Jesus says, "*And every one who has left houses or brothers or sisters or father or mother or wife or children or lands, for My name's sake, shall receive a hundredfold, and inherit eternal life*" (Matthew 19:29). If you will drop your goods on this side of the door and go through the *eye of the needle*, He'll return them to you on the other side, one hundredfold!

Love Thy Neighbor as Thyself

Matthew 22:36-40:

> *Teacher, which is the great commandment in the law?*
>
> *Jesus said to him, You shall love the Lord your God with all your heart, with all your soul, and with all your mind.*
>
> *This is the first and great commandment.*
>
> *And the second is like it, You shall love your neighbor as yourself.*
>
> *On these two commandments hang all the law and the prophets.*

Jesus was saying, "If you can keep these two commandments, you can keep them all."

Romans 13:8:

> *Owe no one anything except to love one another, for he who loves another has fulfilled the law.*

Galatians 5:14:

> *For all the law is fulfilled in one word, even in this: You shall love your neighbor as yourself.*

James 2:8-9:

> *If you really fulfill the royal law according to the Scripture, You shall love your neighbor as yourself, you do well:*

But if you show partiality, you commit sin, and are convicted by the law as transgressors.

Can you see why love is so important to your faith? If you are not walking in love, you are transgressing, and faith cannot work in the life of a transgressor. Love must work with faith to keep out fear and sin so you can fulfill the law and walk in the blessings of God. Romans 5:5 says the love of God *has been poured out in our hearts by the Holy Spirit who was given to us.* Once the Holy Spirit moves into your heart, the law of love is fulfilled!

3
STRONG FAITH

Being Fully Persuaded

Romans 4:20-21:

> *He* (Abraham) *staggered not at the promise of God through unbelief; but was strong in faith, giving glory to God;*
>
> *And being fully persuaded that, what He had promised, He was able also to perform.* (KJV)

Verse 21 gives us the definition of strong faith: *Being fully persuaded that what God has promised He is also able to perform.* Abraham learned that not only is God *able* to perform His promises, He is *willing!* Some of us have recognized that

God is able to heal, deliver, and provide, but have missed the fact that He is also *willing* to do so! We often talk about God's *ability* to perform His promises, but rarely talk of His *willingness*.

Abraham discovered the combination for strong faith: Recognizing both God's ability and willingness to bring His promises to pass. This is the necessary combination for strong faith. Without both, we have no basis for our faith. Just knowing God is *able*, will not bring His promises to pass. Neither will just knowing He is *willing*. It takes both.

Suppose a very wealthy person stood before a group of twenty people and said, "I am *able* to give each one of you fifty thousand dollars." No one would doubt his ability, but neither would anyone get very excited. Just because he is *able* doesn't mean he is *willing*. Ability alone is no basis for faith.

Similarly, suppose a poor person says to that same group, "My great desire is to give you each fifty thousand dollars." This person is certainly *willing* to give, but has no *ability* to give. Willingness alone is no basis for faith. Both ability and willingness must be combined to have faith.

Verse 21 says of Abraham, "*And being* FULLY PERSUADED *that what He* (God) *promised, He was able also to perform.*" You will never know if you are fully persuaded until you're confronted with a situation that puts your faith to the test.

Faith is a growing process and so is the knowledge of God's ability and willingness to fulfill His promises. One of the reasons the world has such a wrong picture of God is because through the years people have expressed God's *ability* to fulfill His promises while leaving out His *willingness*.

Great Faith

Matthew 8:5-10, 13:

> *Now when Jesus was entered into Capernaum, a centurion came to Him, pleading with Him,*

Saying, Lord, my servant is lying at home paralyzed, dreadfully tormented.

And Jesus said to him, I will come and heal him.

The centurion answered and said, Lord, I am not worthy that you should come under my roof. But only speak a word, and my servant will be healed.

For I also am a man under authority, having soldiers under me: and I say to this one, Go, and he goes; and to another, Come, and he comes; and to my servant, Do this, and he does it.

When Jesus heard it, he marveled, and said to those who followed, Assuredly, I say to you, I have not found such great faith, not in Israel.

> *Then Jesus said to the centurion, Go your way; and as you believed, so let it be done for you. And his servant was healed that same hour.*

I believe the theme of God's ability and willingness runs throughout Matthew chapter 8. The Jews thought they had an automatic "in" with God because they were born Jews. They didn't realize physical birth means nothing to the Lord. What is most important to Him is the new birth. This centurion expressed faith and that is what Jesus had been looking for.

The story of the centurion is told twice in the Bible and the two accounts seem to contradict one another. One account says the centurion came to Jesus, the other says the centurion sent his friends, *the elders of the Jews* (Luke 7:3). This centurion never left his house. In the day in which this was written, when one man sent another out in his name, it was just as if that man actually went himself.

The centurion sent representatives in his name.

Similarly, we have been sent in the name of Jesus. When we speak, it is as if Jesus is speaking. Jesus told his disciples, "*...these sign will follow those who believe:* IN MY NAME *I they will cast out demons...they will lay hands on the sick, and they will recover*" (Mark 16:17-18). Do you think a demon is cast out because you're such a hot shot? No. He comes out because you use the Name of Jesus. When someone is healed because you lay hands on them, it is because of that Name.

Jesus acknowledged the centurion for his great faith. Just as Abraham was fully persuaded he would have a son, this man was fully persuaded Jesus would heal his servant.

A Full Day's Journey

Imagine for a moment, you are one of Jesus' disciples listening as the centurion's representatives approached

Jesus. "Lord, we have a master who is a centurion. He stayed behind, but he has a servant who is very ill. Will you please come and heal his servant?" I can picture one disciple turning to another disciple and saying, "I'm sure Jesus is going to tell these guys to bring the sick servant to His healing meeting. With all the multitudes He's been dealing with, I'm sure He doesn't have time to travel just to pray for this servant." However, to the surprise of the disciples, Jesus said, "I will go to the servant and pray for him." The centurion didn't live just a few miles away. His hometown was twenty miles from where Jesus and His disciples were—a full day's journey!

Once they arrive in Capernaum, the centurion says, "You don't even need to come to my house. Just speak the word and my servant will be healed." i can imagine the disciples starting to grumble, "You mean we walked all this way, and now the guy says, 'Don't come'?" As they are grumbling, Jesus says to them, "Guys, this is great faith in operation."

The Centurion's Perspective

The centurion was in his house and his servant was dying. He wanted to help this servant, but didn't know what to do or how to help him. Someone must have told him about Jesus. "I saw a man named Jesus who has been praying for people. A blind man's eyes were opened and he could see. A deaf man's ears were opened and he could hear. A woman who was bent over for years can now stand upright." Based on the reports about Jesus, the centurion sent his servants, knowing Jesus was *able* to heal. However, realizing Jesus had walked twenty miles just to heal his servant, the centurion knew Jesus was *willing*.

I can picture the centurion's servants saying, "Sir, the elders of the Jews are coming and there are several other men with them. Sir, Jesus is with them!" As the centurion runs to the window and sees Jesus he says, "Not only is Jesus *able* to heal, He is *willing!* Tell Him not to come any further. Just speak the word and my servant will be healed!"

Jesus said to His disciples, "This is the faith I have been looking for. This centurion's faith is great, just as Abraham's was. I haven't found this kind of faith even in My own hometown!"

Jesus has not changed since the day the centurion's servant was healed. He is not only *able* to meet your need, He is also *willing!*

4

The Final Destination of Our Faith

Regardless of where you are in your walk of faith, the principles of faith never change. Your parents may have purchased your first car or maybe you worked many hours and saved for weeks and weeks until you had enough money to buy your first car. Either way, more than likely it wasn't a luxury vehicle. It probably didn't matter to you because it got you where you needed to go. Today you may own a car that is more technologically advanced than that first car you owned, but the principle utilizing the vehicle hasn't changed. You still have to get behind the wheel, put the key in the ignition, and drive to your destination.

The same principle applies to faith. Our faith has probably grown and matured since we were first born again, but the principles of faith have not changed. Often, as Christians we spend time studying, examining, and complicating our lives and forget about the foundations of our faith.

Having Your Senses Exercised

Galatians 3:1-5:

> *O foolish Galatians! Who has bewitched you, that you should not obey the truth, before whose eyes Jesus Christ was clearly portrayed among you as crucified?*
>
> *This only I want to learn from you: Did you receive the Spirit by the works of the law, or by the hearing of faith?*

> *Are you so foolish? Having begun in the Spirit, are you now being made perfect by the flesh?*
>
> *Have you suffered so many things in vain? If indeed it was in vain.*
>
> *Therefore He who supplies the Spirit to you, and works miracles among you, does he do it by the works of the law, or by the hearing of faith?*

The Galatians saints had become sidetracked and Paul reminded them that no matter how many years they had been born again, regardless of the amount of Word they had learned, the principles of faith were still the same as the faith that caused them to be born again: *Believe in your heart and confess with your mouth* (Romans 10:9-10).

Living a consistent life of faith means believing God's Word over what our natural senses and reason are speaking to us. Living by faith is not dismissing our senses, our natural mind, or our ability to think and reason. Living by faith requires reprogramming our senses, reprogramming our thinking, and reprogramming our reasoning with the Word of God.

Hebrews 5:14 says, "*...by reason of use*" we have our "*senses exercised to discern both good and evil.*" (KJV) God doesn't want us to completely discard our senses. He wants us to retrain ourselves so everything we think and do, every reaction we have, is based on the Word of God and becomes a lifestyle. The key to the Christian life is the renewing or reprogramming of the mind to think the way God thinks.

The new birth was the first time we exercised godly faith. We had to believe what God said over our natural reasoning. We did not see Jesus die on the cross with our own eyes. We did not see Him resurrected from the dead. Yet, we chose to confess with our mouth Jesus Christ as our Lord and Savior according to Romans 10:9-10 and it resulted in our salvation and us becoming the righteousness of God in Christ Jesus!

The Operation of Faith Never Changes

Since the time of our new birth, we have probably studied faith, grown in our understanding of faith, and have a greater comprehension of the life of faith. These things are all good, but God intends for our faith is to be used and exercised in our daily life.

Galatians 3:1-4 looks back on our salvation. Verse 2 talks about being saved by faith. Verse 3 speaks of growing up in faith. Verse 4 talks about using faith in the midst of tribulation. However, verse 5 looks to the future. God still desires to perform miracles on a daily basis; today, tomorrow, next week—it will never change. We should know more about the Word and living by faith tomorrow than we do today, but no matter how much we learn, the operation of faith never changes.

The reason we clean spark plugs, change the oil, and maintain the engine in our car is so we can drive it! The same is true of faith. Even though we may examine it, the purpose for studying faith is to use it. We may examine whether or not we have unforgiveness in our heart. We may search to see if there is any doubt or unbelief, but the whole reason we examine these things is so we can put our faith into practice.

Heroes of Faith Were Human

Aside from Jesus and the Apostle Paul in the New Testament, Abraham is probably the greatest hero of faith found in the Bible. Even those in other false religions look up to Abraham as a great man of faith and want to associate the roots of their religion with him.

Throughout the ages, there has been a tendency to deify the lives of people who are mentioned in the Bible yet, the Bible never does this. There is nothing wrong with examining the lives of the men and women mentioned in the Bible. We can learn from the things they did right and also learn from the mistakes they made. If the Bible were not inspired by the Holy Spirit, we probably would never have known about anyone's mistakes! If David had written the Bible, we probably would have heard about him killing the bear and the lion as a shepherd boy, slaying the giant, Goliath, with a stone, defeating the Philistines, and all the other wonderful victories he had in his life. However, we probably would never have heard about Bathsheba, Uriah, or any of the other mistakes and failures David accumulated during his lifetime.

King Solomon was the wisest man found in the Old Testament and also the wealthiest. People came from other nations just to see his wealth. Yet, there is an entire book dedicated to Solomon's failures: Ecclesiastes. By reading the book of Ecclesiastes we learn what it is like to be out of fellowship with God, what it's like to live in carnality as Solomon did for most of his life.

Abraham Did Things His Own Way

David and Solomon are not the only people found in the Bible who tried to do things their own way. Abraham also tried to do things his way instead of God's. Genesis 15:6 says, "*And he* (Abraham) *believed in the Lord, and he* (God) *accounted it to him for righteousness.*" As soon as Abraham trusted in God, God immediately saw him as righteous. However, even though Abraham started out in simple faith, he complicated everything. He obeyed God and left his home country, but he took his father and his nephew, Lot, along with him. Abraham and his wife, Sarah, eventually went to Egypt where they met Hagar. They brought Hagar back with them and Ishmael was the result. For some twenty-five years, Abraham tried to solve his own problems. Abraham couldn't save himself, only God could save him. Yet Abraham thought like so many Christians still think today. Somehow we think God saved us so we can deliver ourselves from that point on!

You cannot save yourself. You cannot keep yourself. In your own strength, you cannot be spiritual from day-to-day. Having begun in the Spirit, you are *not* now made perfect in the flesh. Having begun in the Spirit, you must now *remain* in the Spirit. For years, Abraham kept going in circles. Once in awhile he would trust God and God would deliver him, but the next time he would say, "Lord, I'll solve it myself." Abraham piled up such a string of failures and weights in his life, which were a result of his own choices, that he finally surrendered completely to the Lord and told Sarah, "We are going to trust God for the promise of a son to come to pass." Isaac was finally born and Abraham's faith grew so strong, he was willing to sacrifice the son God had promised him so many years before. A man who once depended on himself had grown in faith so when God spoke to him, he was quick to obey and do what God was asking him to do.

Abraham is an example for us. You may look at yourself and recognize the reason you're not where you should be today is your fault, not God's. We serve a God who is ready to forgive you if you'll ask Him, and He will restore all the years that have been lost. What He did for Abraham, He will do for you. Maybe you're thinking, "God may forgive me, but I've lived too long my own way. I think it's too late for God's promises to come to pass." As long as you are still alive, God can revive those promises and restore what has been lost. He redeems the time!

Why God Chose Abraham

Genesis 12 reveals why God chose Abraham. God spoke to Abraham not long after the Tower of Babel when He had scattered the people and made different languages because of their sin. Since the people no longer spoke the same language and could not understand one another, nations formed. However, God decided to start His own nation. The other nations began naturally, but this nation would begin supernaturally. God chose Abraham. He didn't choose Abraham because he was perfect. God saw something in Abraham's life that caused Him to choose Abraham.

Genesis 12:1-3:

> *Now the Lord had said to Abram: Get out of you country, from your family, and from thy father's house, to a land that I will show you:*
>
> *I will make you a great nation; I will* BLESS *you, and make your name great; and you shall be a* BLESSING*:*

> *I will* BLESS *those who* BLESS *you, and I will curse him who curses you; and in you all the families of the earth shall be* BLESSED.

Notice the number of times *bless, blessed*, or *blessing* are used in this passage. God is the author of all blessings. Every good and perfect gift comes down from above. The second half of verse 3 was quoted in Galatians 3:8, "*...in you all the families of the earth shall be blessed.*" The reason God wanted to use Abraham is found in verse 2, "*...and you shall be a blessing.*" God said, "Abraham, the reason I am going to bless you is because I know you will turn around and be a blessing."

Before Abraham stepped into the promised land, before he ever saw gold or silver, before Abraham ever saw a child come along, before he ever received any spiritual or natural blessings from God, God said, "Abraham, before I ever bless you I am telling you the reason I will bless you: I see in you that you are going to be quick to give. I know when I give to you, the end result is you're going to bless others. You are going to be a channel I can use!"

Why Are We Here?

Why are we here? What is the destination of our faith? Where does God want to lead us? God wants us to reach the place Abraham was. God wants us to be just like Him. Aren't you glad God doesn't hoard up His treasures in heaven? Aren't you glad God looked toward you when it came to salvation? Aren't you glad He has poured His blessings of peace, healing, prosperity and so many others to you since you were born again? I can tell you, your name is attached to many more blessings in the days to come.

God's desire is for us to act just like Him. He wants us to imitate Him. In this earth, the only God some people are going to see is through us. The only scripture they are going to read is through our life. The Bible calls our lives "living epistles." When people look at us, they should see the character of God. Although we still live in a flesh and blood body, the longer we walk with Him, the more people should see traces of His love, forgiveness, generosity, mercy, His character manifested through our lives.

Abraham's Generosity

Abraham was generous with everyone around him, even his nephew, Lot. Even though Lot was extremely self-centered, this did not hinder Abraham's generosity toward him. Abraham didn't qualify his giving. He continued to bless Lot in spite of his selfishness. There came a day when Abraham and Lot were so blessed, their flocks and herds and possessions began to run into each other. You couldn't tell which herd was Lot's and which was Abraham's because they were both so blessed. To alleviate strife that was beginning to develop between their families, Abraham told Lot, "You choose whatever land you want to take as yours." Of course, Lot, being an opportunist, chose the absolute best piece of ground available. The problem with his choice is that it faced Sodom, which would eventually be his downfall. Abraham was a giver and he was quick to give. God desires us to have the same attitude Abraham had.

We must ask ourselves a question: What is the destination God wants to bring us to? Is the purpose of faith so I can get a better car, so my bills are paid? That is certainly part of it, but it is only a means to an end. What will you do when your bills are paid and God blesses you with extra money? Will you heap it on yourself or will you say, "Where can I give? Who can I give to? What kind of blessing can I be?"

The Simple Operation of Faith

There are two stories found in the Gospels that demonstrate the simple operation of faith.

Mark 11:1-7:

Now when they drew near Jerusalem, to Bethphage and Bethany, at the mount of Olives, He sent two of His disciples;

And said to them, Go your into the village opposite you; and as soon as you have entered it, you will find a colt tied, on which no one sat. Loose it, and bring it.

And if anyone says to you, Why are you doing this? Say, The Lord has need of it, and immediately he will send it here.

So they went their way, and found the colt tied by the door outside on the street, and they loosed it.

But some of those who stood there said to them, What are you doing, loosing the colt?

And they spoke to them just as Jesus had commanded. So they let them go.

Then they brought the colt to Jesus and threw their clothes on it, and He sat on it.

Mark 14:13-16:

And he sent out two of his disciples, and said to them, Go into the city, and a man will meet you carrying a pitcher of water; follow him.

Where he goes in, say to the master of the house, The Teacher says, Where is the guest room in which I may eat the Passover with My disciples?

Then he will show you a large upper room, furnished and

> *prepared; there make ready for us.*
>
> *So his disciples went out, and came into the city, and found it just as He had said to them; and they prepared the Passover.*

These events both took place just before the crucifixion of Jesus. Although the disciples had questioned Jesus many times during their three years with Him, in these two cases they simply obeyed.

In the first case, Jesus told the disciples "Go find a colt." He told them exactly where the colt would be found. They were questioned just like Jesus told them they would be questioned. Jesus told them what to say when they were questioned about taking the colt, they obeyed, and delivered the colt to Jesus.

In the second case, just a few days later, Jesus was preparing for the Passover. He sent two disciples to find a man carrying a water pitcher. Jesus said, "Look for a man with a pitcher of water and follow him. When the man with the pitcher goes to the doorway, ask him if we can use the upper room and he will let us." It came to pass just like Jesus said it would. In both cases, I want you to notice how quick the disciples were to obey. Whether the Holy Spirit speaks something or you find it in the Word, simple obedience is important to the operation of faith.

Do What He Tells You to Do

Think about the first miracle Jesus ever performed. Jesus and his mother were at a wedding and they had run out of wine. Jesus told the men "Go fill the water pots with water." I'm sure they looked at each other and thought, "Who is this guy?" Mary said, "Just do what He tells you to do." Jesus turned the water into wine. Mary's instruction to the men was a great admonition to us in our walk of faith. If God asks you to do something in faith, don't argue, don't reason, just do what He has asked you to do! There is nothing wrong with questioning as long as you are obedient. If questioning leads to disobedience, something is wrong. You may have questioned God's will and direction for your life over the years, but obeyed anyway and discovered God was right!

One thing I want to point out about these two stories is the provision was there before the disciples ever went. The colt was already tied and waiting for the disciples. I wonder how many days before this the Lord arranged everything so when the disciples arrived they would find the colt. If God gives you something to do, you can be assured the provisions have already been made. God doesn't work last minute. He doesn't say, "Oh, by the way Holy Spirit, we better get this thing worked out quickly because my servant is on the way!" God had things worked out long before He ever told you to go!

Another point I want to make is the importance of obeying God when He speaks. God's timing is important because He has prepared that colt and it's waiting for you. He has prepared that man with the pitcher of water to cross your path at just the right moment. Timing is so important.

Be A Water Pot Carrier

God has many water pots ahead for you, but let me ask you a question: Is there anything better than meeting a man with a water pot? Yes, being the person with the water pot! Where did this man get his water pot? One day he needed water, his water pot need was met, and he used the water pot of his provision to begin meeting the needs of other people!

Why did God choose Abraham? He knew when He gave Abraham his water pot, Abraham would begin looking for people to bless. The reason God blesses us is not just so we can walk away with our need met saying, "Glory to God! Is there another water pot for me? How about tomorrow? Will I get another water pot?" God doesn't bless us so we can think to ourselves *God's met this need. How's He going to meet my next need?* This is not the attitude God is looking for. He is looking for someone who will say, "God, thank you for sending a water pot my way. Now I'm going to carry one so I can be used to meet someone else's need for a water pot! You've met my needs, now I can bless others. You have blessed me so I can be a blessing!"

This should be the final destination of our faith: *To be a blessing even as we have been blessed!*

Books by Bob Yandian

Decently and In Order
Ephesians
Family Defined
Fellowshipping with God
Forever Changed
From Just Enough to Overflowing
God's Word to Pastors
Grace: From Here to Eternity
How Deep are the Stripes?
Joel
Leadership Secrets of David the King
One Flesh
One Nation Under God
Proverbs
Resurrection
Righteousness: God's Gift to You
Spirit Controlled Life
The Fullness of the Spirit
Unlimited Partnership
Understanding the End Times
You Have a Ministry
Philippians Notes
Colossians Notes
James Notes
Acts Notes Pt 1

How to Contact Bob Yandian Ministries

Phone:

1-800-284-0595
Local: (918) 250-2207

Mailing Address:

Bob Yandian Ministries
PO Box 55236
Tulsa, OK 74155

BobYandian.com

PRAYER OF SALVATION

God loves you—no matter who you are, no matter what your past. God loves you so much that He gave His one and only begotten Son for you. The Bible tells us that "...whoever believes in Him shall not perish but have eternal life" (John 3:16 NIV). Jesus laid down His life and rose again so that we could spend eternity with Him in heaven and experience His absolute best on earth. If you would like to receive Jesus into your life, say the following prayer out loud and mean it from your heart.

Heavenly Father, I come to You admitting that I am a sinner. Right now, I choose to turn away from sin, and I ask You to cleanse me of all unrighteousness. I believe that Your Son, Jesus, died on the cross to take away my sins. I also believe that He rose again from the dead so that I might be forgiven of my sins and made righteous through faith in Him. I call upon the name of Jesus Christ to be the Savior and Lord of my life. Jesus, I choose to follow You and ask that You fill me with the power of the Holy Spirit. I declare that right now I am a child of God. I am free from sin and full of the righteousness of God. I am saved in Jesus' name. Amen.

If you prayed this prayer to receive Jesus Christ as your ior for the first time, please contact us on the Web at w.**harrisonhouse.com** to receive a free book.

Or you may write to us at

rison House • P.O. Box 35035 • Tulsa, Oklahoma 74153